AhaHAHaheH

For Mum, Dad, Peter and Rob.

Printed in the UK by Northend Creative Print, Sheffield on FSC® certified paper
ISBN: 978 0 9934701 0 3

To order and find out more visit www.littlehyenapress.com

FSC
www.fsc.org
MIX
Paper from
responsible sources
FSC® C019447

Little Hyena laughed all the time ...

naHaHahaHEhehe

but he laughed at *all* the wrong things.

Little Hyena thought it was funny when
Snake got himself tied up in knots.

He didn't think to help,
he just giggled.

Next Little Hyena saw Tortoise struggling to get to his feet ...

but he just watched him rolling around
and chuckled.

Then Little Hyena saw Elephant's big bottom
was stuck between the trees.

He laughed ...

and laughed ...

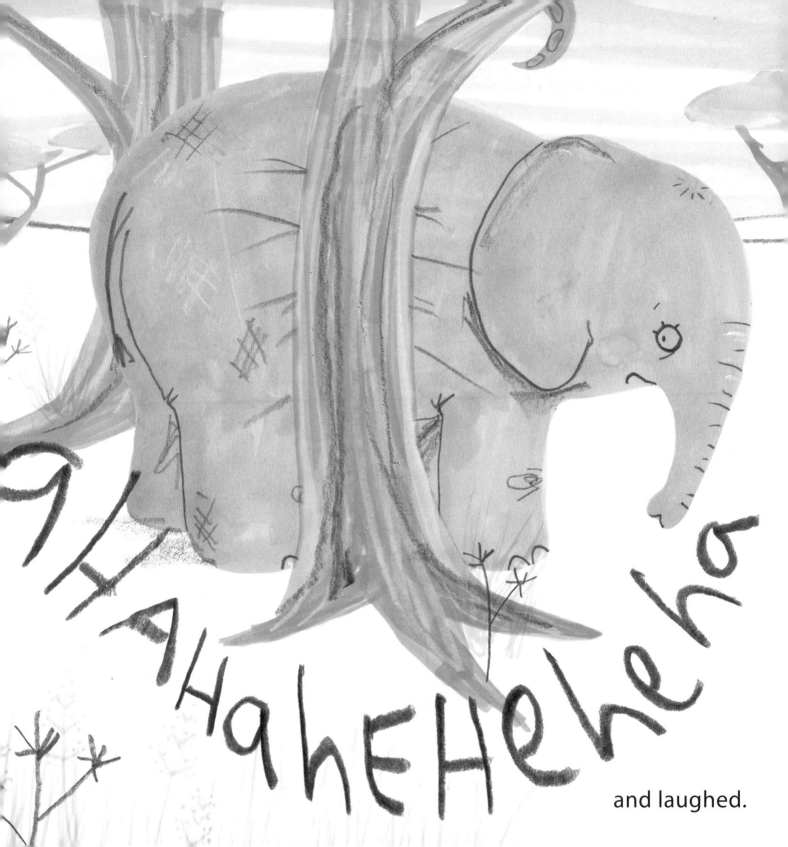

and laughed.

He was so busy laughing ...

he didn't look where he was going!

cried Little Hyena, as he skidded ...

... straight into
Elephant's big bottom ...

... and bounced off ...

weeeee.....

shaking the trees, which sent Elephant sliding,
and Snake flying through the air!

Elephant slid along the ground ...

and crashed into Tortoise!

Luckily they all landed safely!

But where was
Little Hyena?

Just then they heard Little Hyena in the distance, calling for help.

He had bounced straight into a water hole!

The friends all worked together
to help pull Little Hyena to safety.

Little Hyena was very sorry for laughing at them ...

and he thanked his
new friends for
helping him.

Little Hyena and his new friends told their funniest jokes ...

and laughed together
until the sun went down!

heHeHeHAHaA
ahA
hahAhah
wahAhA
TEtsse

nAHaHa HaheHEHe

AhaHAHaHEH
ag

eeeheehee

haHAH qOOAHAhq

We love poo!